# MONSTER
## Needs One More!

pictures by
### Natalie Marshall

BLUE APPLE

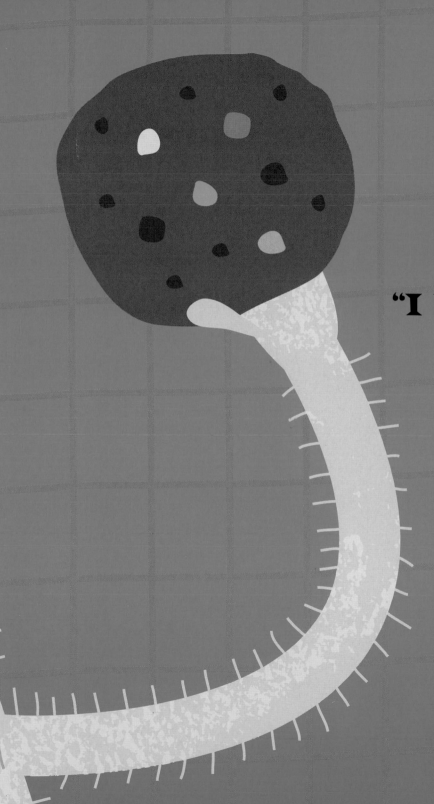

This hungry
monster says:
"I have ONE cookie.
I need
one more!"

"ANOTHER cookie to chew!"

"I had ONE. Now I have TWO!"

"**ANOTHER** balloon just for me!"

"I had **TWO.** Now I have **THREE!**"

This grumpy monster says:
"I have **THREE** apples.
I must have
one more!"

**"ANOTHER apple! Here's one more!"**

**"I had THREE. Now I have FOUR!"**

This sad monster says:
"I have FOUR beach balls.
I need one more!"

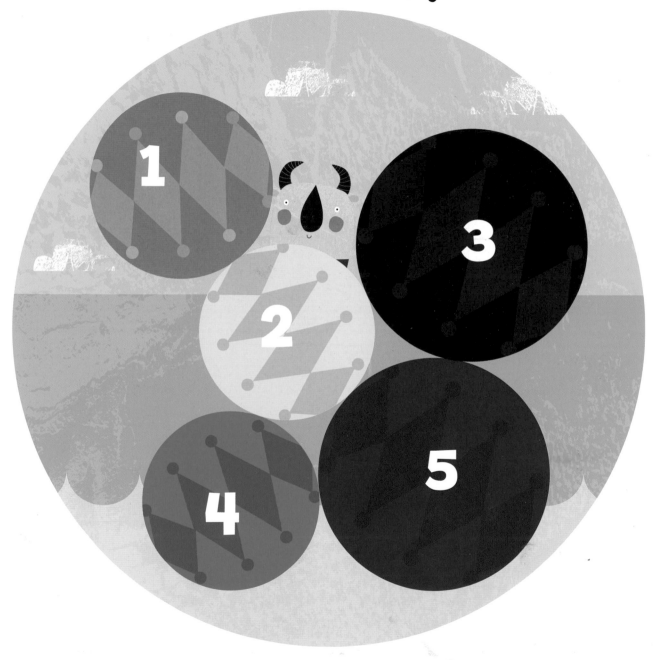

"**ANOTHER** beach ball!
Like the water? Can you dive?"

"I had **FOUR**. Now I have **FIVE!**"

This grabby
monster says:
"I have FIVE
strawberries.

I need one more!"

This grouchy
monster says:
"I have SIX crackers.
I need one more!"

**"SO MANY crackers! Eight? Eleven?"**

**"I had SIX. Now I have SEVEN!"**

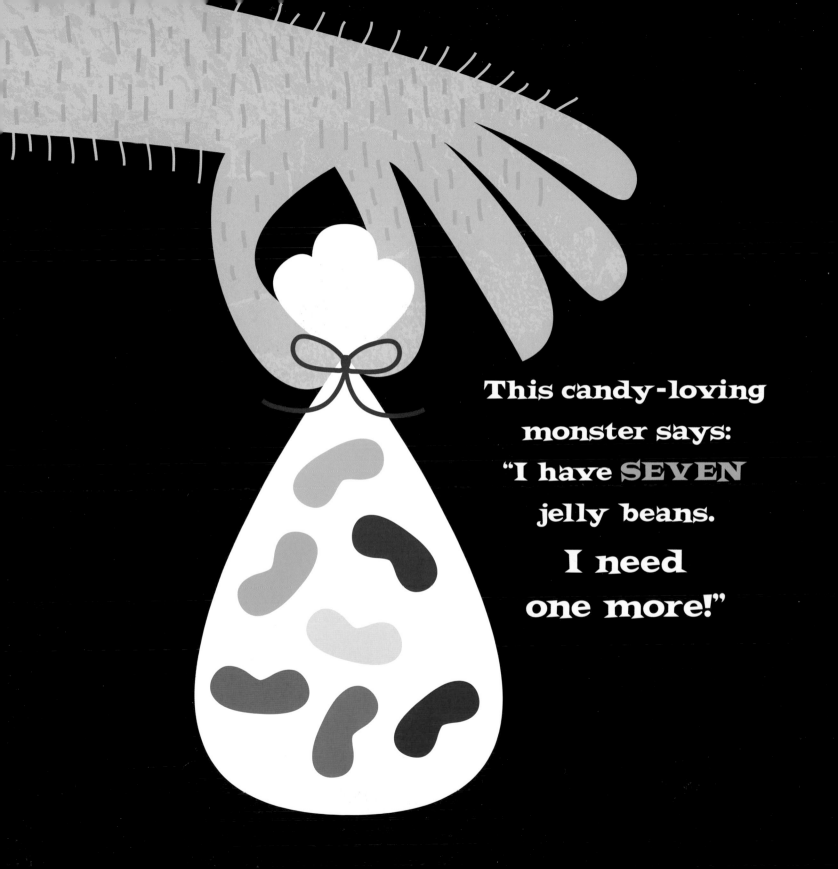

This candy-loving
monster says:
"I have SEVEN
jelly beans.
I need
one more!"

"LOTS of jelly beans! Isn't that great? I had SEVEN. Now I have EIGHT!"

This sleepy monster says:
"I have **EIGHT** teddy bears. **I need one more!**"

"A gold bear! That's so fine!"

"I had **EIGHT**. Now I have **NINE!**"

Then this sleepy monster says:
"I have **NINE** goodnight kisses. **I want MORE!**"

"MORE! MORE! Mama, kiss me again!"

"I had NINE. Now I have TEN!"

"I'm cozy! I'm snug!
Now all I need is ..."

# "One BIG hug!"